The Fairiest Fairy

To all my lovely family — A. B.

For Maddie, with love — R. B.

Text copyright © 2015 by Anne Booth

Illustrations copyright © 2015 by Rosalind Beardshaw

Nosy Crow and its logos are trademarks of Nosy Crow Ltd. Used under license.

First U.S. edition 2016

Library of Congress Catalog Card Number 2015941690

ISBN 978-0-7636-8659-8

16 17 18 19 20 21 FGF 10 9 8 7 6 5 4 3 2 1

Printed in Shenzhen, Guangdong, China

This book was typeset in Tryst.

The illustrations were done in mixed media.

Nosy Crow

an imprint of

Candlewick Press

99 Dover Street

Somerville, Massachusetts 02144

www.nosycrow.com

www.candlewick.com

The Fairiest Fairy

Anne Booth

illustrated by

Rosalind Beardshaw

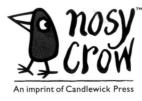

An imprint of Candlewick Press

Betty was a fairy who just **never** got things right. She was **always** in a muddle though she tried with all her might.

And when she went to Fairy School,
she did her **very** best.
But fairy wings are **tricky** . . .

when you're

putting on

a vest.

Her pirouettes were wobbly,
though most enthusiastic,
and no one else's magic wand
was tied on with elastic.

"What shall we do with Betty?" her fairy teacher cried.
"She's such a messy muddle!" and she shook her head and sighed.

One day, Miss Petal clapped her hands.
"Now, fairies, listen well!
Today's a **most** important day –
it's time for your
first spell."

"The first thing that a fairy learns is lots and lots of fun.
Let's scatter all the dewdrops so they sparkle in the sun!"

"The **other** fairies get it right," said Betty, feeling sad.

"My dewdrops just make **puddles** since my sprinkling is so bad."

Then Betty heard a rabbit cry—
he sounded SO forlorn.
And in his little paw she found
a **very** nasty thorn.

She pulled it out and bathed his foot
in one of her dew puddles.
Then dried the
little rabbit's tears . . .

and gave him
lots of cuddles.

"**Thank you!**" said the rabbit. "Oh, you are so **very kind.**
Now I can hop with **all** my friends and not get left behind!"

That day at school the fairies learned another special power.
Miss Petal taught them morning spells to wake up **every** flower.

The other fairies
waved their wands
and each bud
opened up . . .

while Betty found a baby
bird behind a buttercup.

"I'm hiding," said the little bird.
"I'm much too scared to fly!"

But Betty said,
"I'm sure you're brave,"
and showed him how to try.

"Oh, thank you!" said the blackbird,
and he flapped his wings and flew.
"You helped me find my courage –
now just see what I can do!"

Just then the rain came pouring down
from dark clouds overhead.

"It's time to paint
some rainbows now,"
Miss Petal quickly said.

But Betty's flying was so slow,
she started **very** late.

She had to **rush** her rainbow,
and it got in **quite** a state.

Betty felt so glum she crept
away into the flowers.
But then a little voice said,
"I've been stuck in here for **hours!**

My laces are all tangled up.
I don't know **what** to do!"
"I'll work it out," said Betty.
"I'll **soon** untangle you."

"Oh, thank you!" said the butterfly.
"It's very clear to me
that you're the **smartest** fairy
I could ever hope to see."

All week the fairies practiced
waking flowers, sprinkling dew,
and painting **pretty** rainbows
with red and green and blue.

But little messy Betty had a
brokenhearted cry.
"I'm **always** in a muddle,
even though I try and try."

Each year the fairy king and queen
arranged a Fairy Ball
and chose from all the fairies who's
the fairiest of them all.

But Betty whispered to her friends,
"I can't do anything.
I just can't do spells well enough to
show the queen and king . . .

I have to scatter dewdrops but my
sprinkling is no good,
and I can't wake up the flowers
as a fairy really should.

My rainbows are too wobbly
and all messy at the ends."
"Oh, please don't worry, Betty.
We can help you," said her friends.

First Rabbit had a **bright** idea.
"Now, Betty, hold on tight!
We'll scatter all the dewdrops
as I skip from left to right."

"Bravo! Bravo!" the king exclaimed.
"Well done!" agreed the queen.
"This is the sparkliest dewdrop dance
that we have **ever** seen."

"Oh, thank you, Rabbit," Betty said,
"for such a happy dance.
Without your lovely leaps and bounds,
I didn't have a chance!"

Then Blackbird said,
"To wake the flowers,
just listen to my song . . .

I'll teach you how to whistle it —
it won't take very long."

"Oh, Betty!" said the king and queen.
"You whistle like a bird.
We think your waking-up tune is
the **loveliest** we've heard."

"**Thank you,** Blackbird,"
Betty said. "It's all because of you.
You taught me to be brave
and how to try out something new."

For painting rainbows Butterfly
knew just the thing to do.
"Match the colors on my wings,
from red and green to blue."

"How **beautiful**," the queen exclaimed.
"It's **lovely!**" said the king.
"Your rainbow's truly wonderful—
a **really** gorgeous thing."

Betty blushed and thanked her friend, a bright smile on her face.
"Look! Every single color's in exactly the right place!"

The king said, "Fairies, gather round.
It's time to give the prize.
And when you find out who has won,
it might be a surprise. . . ."

"It's Betty!" said the queen.
"She is so clever, brave, and kind.
She is the Fairiest Fairy
we could ever hope to find."

"Oh, thank you," Betty said.
"The one who's most surprised is me!
I couldn't do a single thing
without my friends, you see."

"But Betty," said the queen,
"you've shown us how to be a **friend,**
and proved that helping others
is what matters in the end."

Then Betty gave a hug to
Rabbit, Bird, and Butterfly,
and all the other fairies cheered
till Betty felt quite shy.

And everyone was happy at the Royal Fairy Ball.
They all agreed that Betty was the Fairiest of Them All.